THE BOXCAR CHILDREN ®

MYSTERY RANCH

Time to Read™ is an early reader program designed to guide children to literacy success regardless of age or grade level. The program's three levels correspond to stages of reading readiness, making book selection straightforward, and assuring that when it's time for a child to read, the right book is waiting.

— Level 1 —

Beginning to Read

- Large, simple type
- Basic vocabulary
- Word repetition
- Strong illustration support

— Level 2 —

Reading with Help

- Short sentences
- Engaging stories
- Simple dialogue
- Illustration support

— Level 3 —

Reading Independently

- Longer sentences
- Harder words
- Short paragraphs
- Increased story complexity

Library of Congress Cataloging-in-Publication data is on file with the publisher.

Copyright © 2019 by Albert Whitman & Company
Hardcover edition first published in the United States of America
in 2019 by Albert Whitman & Company
Paperback edition first published in the United States of America
in 2019 by Albert Whitman & Company
ISBN 978-0-8075-5435-7 (paperback)
ISBN 978-0-8075-5431-9 (ebook)
Printed in China
10 9 8 7 6 5 4 3 2 1 T&N 24 23 22 21 20 19

Cover and interior art by Shane Clester

Visit the Boxcar Children online at www.boxcarchildren.com.
For more information about Albert Whitman & Company,
visit our website at www.albertwhitman.com.

100 Years of Albert Whitman & Company
Celebrate with us in 2019!

THE BOXCAR CHILDREN®

MYSTERY RANCH

Based on the book by
Gertrude Chandler Warner

Albert Whitman & Company
Chicago, Illinois

On the first day of summer,
Benny Alden woke up early.
So did his best friend, Watch.
"Come on, boy!" Benny said.

Henry, Jessie, and Violet
were up too.
Everyone was excited for a
new adventure.

In the kitchen, Grandfather did not look excited.

"What's wrong?" Violet asked.

Grandfather sighed.

"It's my sister, Jane. Her neighbor Sam wrote to me. Your great-aunt is not doing well."

Henry, Jessie, Violet, and Benny
had never met Aunt Jane.
After their parents died,
the children had run away.
For a little while, they had lived
in a boxcar.
Then Grandfather found them.

Now they had a real home.
But they were still learning
about their family.

"Is Aunt Jane sick?" asked Violet.

"I'm afraid she is lonely,"
Grandfather said.

"She lives on a big ranch
all by herself."

Jessie had an idea.

"We could go and visit her!"

"Watch can come too!"
said Benny.

"He makes everybody happier."

Grandfather smiled.

He knew his grandchildren
were very good at cheering
people up.

The next morning, the children got on the train.
It was a long trip.
Benny thought they would never get to Aunt Jane's ranch.

A friendly passenger helped.
He showed Benny where they
were on the map.
"Now entering Wyoming!"
Benny called.

At last, the train pulled into
their stop: Centerville.
Only one other person got off.
It was the man with the map!

"How strange," said Jessie. "We were going to the same place the whole time." "I'm going to call him Mystery Man!" said Benny.

The children met Sam
at the station.
He brought them to
Aunt Jane's ranch.

Henry saw strange stones
by the road.
"This ranch is the only place
I have seen those rocks,"
Sam told him.
Henry wondered what other
surprises might be hidden on
the big ranch.

At the house, Aunt Jane was not in a good mood, just as Grandfather had feared. The children tried to cheer her up.

Jessie told her about the
Mystery Man on the train.
Aunt Jane only frowned.
"He will be gone soon.
No one stays in Centerville
anymore."

Benny had an idea.

"When I'm sad, I give Watch
a big hug," he said.

With that, Watch jumped right
up onto Aunt Jane's bed.

For a moment, Jessie thought
Aunt Jane might be mad.

But then she smiled.

Benny smiled too.

He did not mind sharing
his best friend.

"Let's get to work," Jessie said.
Jessie liked to have things
in order.
She thought it would help
cheer up Aunt Jane.
The children cleaned.

Then they went to buy groceries
for supper.
"I hope we see Mystery Man
in town," said Benny.

But the real mystery was back
at the ranch...

Aunt Jane was out of bed.
But her smile was gone.
"Thank goodness you are back,"
she said.
"Some people were here.
They wanted me to sell
the ranch!"

"Oh no!" said Violet.

"Why would they want that?"

"I don't know," said Aunt Jane.
"But the ranch is not doing well.
If things do not get better,
I may have to sell."

"Don't worry, Aunt Jane,"
Henry said.
"We'll help with the ranch."

The next day, the children
helped with chores.
Jessie got eggs from the chickens.
Henry milked the cow.

Violet and Benny took care
of the horse.

"I'm going to call him Snowball!"
Benny said.

Everyone laughed.

Even Aunt Jane.

Her brother was right.

The children knew just how
to cheer people up.

After doing chores, the Aldens
explored.

The ranch went on and on.

Right up to the mountains.

Violet found wildflowers.

Henry spotted more of the
strange rocks.

But it was Benny who found
the strangest thing...

A little hut!

"Can we stay the night?"
asked Benny.

"Like we did in the boxcar?"
Henry and Jessie were not
so sure.

It was far away from Aunt
Jane's house.

Who had built the strange
little hut?

And what if they came back?

"We had better get back,"
said Jessie.

"Aunt Jane might be missing us."

At supper, Henry asked about
the strange stones.

Aunt Jane smiled.

"Those are very rare," she said.
"My father wanted to mine
and sell them, but we never
found enough."

Henry wanted to ask more
questions.

But he did not want to upset
his aunt.

The next morning, the children showed Sam the little hut.

Sam frowned.

"Someone has been camping here."

"Why would someone stay on Aunt Jane's land?" asked Violet.

"Do you think it was the people who tried to buy the ranch?" asked Henry.

Sam did not have any answers.

But he did know where to go next.

"Sheriff, someone has been
staying on Jane Alden's ranch,"
Sam said.

Henry told the policeman
about all the strange things
they had seen.

But the man did not
look worried.

"I think there is someone you
should meet," he said.

"Mystery Man!" said Benny.
"What are you doing here?"
The man explained.
"My name is Mr. Carter.
Your grandfather sent me.
I came to look at the rocks
on your aunt's ranch.
You see, I sell rocks."
"That's why we got on and off
the train at the same place!"
said Jessie.
"Aunt Jane said there were not
many of those strange rocks,"
said Henry.
Mr. Carter smiled.
He had something to show them.

"These hills are full of those rocks," said Mr. Carter. "But some people found them before I did. They wanted them for themselves. They tried to buy Aunt Jane's ranch."

"Is that who was staying in the little hut?" asked Henry.

"That's right," said Mr. Carter. "But the sheriff and I sent them away."

"Does that mean Jane won't
have to sell her ranch?"
asked Sam.

Mr. Carter nodded.

It meant much more than that.

Over the next few weeks, many
people came to Centerville.
They helped mine and sell
the rocks.
Aunt Jane had all the company
she could want.

There was just one thing missing…

a best friend.

Keep reading with the Boxcar Children!

Henry, Jessie, Violet, and Benny used to live in a Boxcar. Now they have adventures everywhere they go! Adapted from the beloved chapter book series, these early readers allow kids to begin reading with the stories that started it all.

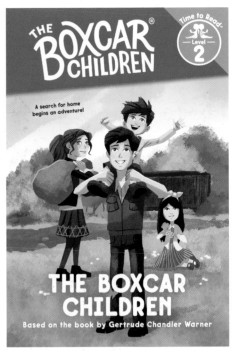

HC 978-0-8075-0839-8 · US $12.99
PB 978-0-8075-0835-0 · US $3.99

HC 978-0-8075-7675-5 · US $12.99
PB 978-0-8075-7679-3 · US $3.99

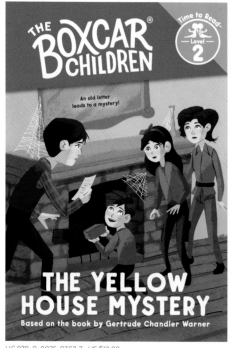

HC 978-0-8075-9367-7 · US $12.99
PB 978-0-8075-9370-7 · US $3.99

GERTRUDE CHANDLER WARNER discovered when she was teaching that many readers who like an exciting story could find no books that were both easy and fun to read. She decided to try to meet this need, and her first book, *The Boxcar Children*, quickly proved she had succeeded.

Miss Warner drew on her own experiences to write the mystery. As a child she spent hours watching trains go by on the tracks opposite her family home. She often dreamed about what it would be like to set up housekeeping in a caboose or freight car—the situation the Alden children find themselves in.

While the mystery element is central to each of Miss Warner's books, she never thought of them as strictly juvenile mysteries. She liked to stress the Aldens' independence and resourcefulness and their solid New England devotion to using up and making do. The Aldens go about most of their adventures with as little adult supervision as possible—something else that delights young readers.

Miss Warner lived in Putnam, Connecticut, until her death in 1979. During her lifetime, she received hundreds of letters from girls and boys telling her how much they liked her books.